CU09767388

The Enchanted Table

and

Other Stories

by
ENID BLYTON

Illustrated by
Lesley Smith

AWARD PUBLICATIONS LIMITED

For further information on Enid Blyton please contact
www.blyton.com

ISBN 0-86163-928-6

This compilation text copyright © 1998 The Enid Blyton Company
Illustrations copyright © 1998 Award Publications Limited

Enid Blyton's signature is a trademark of
The Enid Blyton Company

This edition entitled *The Enchanted Table and Other Stories*
published by permission of The Enid Blyton Company

First published 1998
3rd impression 2000

Published by Award Publications Limited,
27 Longford Street, London NW1 3DZ

Printed in Singapore

CONTENTS

The
Enchanted Table

Once upon a time there was a strange table. It was perfectly round and had four strong legs ending in feet like a lion's paws with claws. Round its edge there was carved a circle of tiny animals – mice, cats, dogs, weasels, rats, pigs and others.

For many years this table stood in the kitchen of a tailor named Snip, and no one knew of its magic powers. Mrs Snip laid a white cloth on it each mealtime and spread it with food and drink. Once a week she polished it. All the little Snip children sat round it three times a day and, dear me, how they kicked it with their fidgety feet! How they stained it when they spilled their tea! How they marked it with their knives, pens and pencils!

One day an old man came to see Snip the tailor. Mrs Snip asked him into the kitchen for a cup of tea, and he suddenly saw the table with its edge of carved animals and its four paws for feet. His eyes opened wide, and he gasped for breath.

"That table!" he cried. "It's magic! Didn't you know?"

"How is it magic?" asked Mrs Snip, not quite believing him at all.

"Look!" cried the old man. He went up to the table and ran his fingers round the carved animals. He pressed first a mouse, then a cat, then a pig, then a weasel, muttering a few strange words as he did so. Then he tapped each of the paw-like feet with his right hand.

"Mercy on us!" cried Mrs Snip, in horror and surprise. "Look at that! Why, it's alive!"

"But wait!" said the old man, in excitement. "Let me show what it can do now!"

He went to the table and put his hands on the middle of it. Then, knocking three

6

times sharply, he said, "Bacon and sausages! New bread! Hot cocoa!"

And, would you believe it, a dish of bacon and sausages, a loaf of new bread, and a jug of hot cocoa suddenly appeared on that strange table!

Mrs Snip couldn't believe her eyes! She sat down on a chair and opened and shut her mouth like a fish, trying to say

something. At last she called the tailor in from his shop. When she told him what had happened he was amazed.

The old man knocked three times on the table again and said, "Two pineapples! Stewed mushrooms!"

Immediately two large pineapples arrived, and a heap of stewed mushrooms planted themselves in the middle of the dish of bacon and sausages. They smelled very nice.

"Can we eat these things?" asked Mr Snip at last.

"Of course," said the old man. They all sat down and began to eat. My, how delicious everything was! The table kept quite still, except that once it held out a paw to the fire and frightened the tailor so much that he swallowed a whole mouthful at once and nearly choked.

"This table is worth a lot of money," said the old man. "You should sell it, Snip. It's hundreds of years old. It was made by the gnome Brinnen, in a cave in the heart of the mountain. How did you come to have it?"

"Oh, it belonged to my father, and to his father, and to his father; in fact, it has been in our family for ages," said the tailor. "But I didn't know it was magic."

"I expect someone forgot how to set the spell working," said the old man. "Look, I'll show you what I did. First you press this animal – then you press this one – and then this – and this – and all the time you say some magic words, which I will whisper into your ear for fear someone hears them."

He whispered. The tailor listened in delight.

"And then," said the old man, "just put your hands in the middle of the table – so – and think what food you want. Then rap smartly three times on the top of the table and call out for what you'd like!"

"Marvellous!" said the tailor, rubbing his hands together. "Wonderful! But I shan't sell my table, friend. No, it has been in my family so long that I could not part with it. I will keep it and let it provide food for me and my family."

"Well, make sure you treat it kindly," said the old man. "It has feelings, you

know. Treat it kindly. It likes a good home. And don't forget to say those magic words once a week."

"Come and dine with us each Sunday," said the tailor. "If it hadn't been for you we should never have found out about the magic."

Well, at first all the tailor's children and friends couldn't say enough about that marvellous table. They simply delighted in rapping on it and ordering meals. It didn't matter what they asked for – it came. Even when Amelia Snip, the eldest child, rapped and asked for ice-cream pickles they appeared on the table in an instant.

What parties the Snips gave! Roasted chickens, legs of pork, suet puddings, mince-pies, apple tarts, sugar biscuits, six different sorts of cheese – everything was there and nobody ever went short.

The table seemed quite content, except that it would keep walking over to the fire, and sometimes it would stroke someone's leg and make that guest jump nearly out of his skin.

But one day the table became impatient. Six little Snip children sat round it and they were very fidgety. Amelia kicked one table-leg. Albert kicked another. Harriet spilt her lemonade over it and made it sticky. Paul cut a tiny hole in it with his new penknife. Susan scratched it with her fingernails. And Bobbo swung his legs up high and kicked the underneath of the table very hard indeed.

The table suddenly lost its temper. It lifted up a paw and smacked Bobbo hard on his leg.

"Ooh!" cried Bobbo, slipping down from his chair in a hurry. "Horrid table! It slapped me!"

"How dare you slap my brother!" cried Amelia, and kicked the table-leg hard. It immediately lifted up its paw, put out its claws, and scratched her like a cat!

"Ow!" cried Amelia, and she ran to the shop, howling. Soon the tailor and his wife came back with her and the tailor scolded the table.

But instead of listening humbly, the

table put up a big paw and slapped Mr Snip! Then it got up and walked over to the fire.

"How many times have I told you that you are not to stand so close to the fire?" scolded Mrs Snip. "No one can sit at you if you do that. It's too hot."

The table ran up to Mrs Snip and with two of its great paws it pushed her into a chair. Then it shook one of its paws at her crossly and went back to the fire again. Mrs Snip was very angry.

"Ho!" she said. "So that's how you're feeling, is it? Well, I'll give you some work to do."

She went over to it and rapped smartly on the top three times, calling out, "Roast beef! Roast pork! Roast mutton! Steak-and-kidney pie! Suet roll! Jam sandwich! Currant cake! Plum pudding!" and so on and so on, everything she could think of! The table soon groaned under the weight of all the food she called for, and its four legs almost bent under their burden.

"There!" said the tailor's wife. "That

will punish you for your spitefulness!"

But the table had had enough of the Snip family. It had never liked them, for they were mean and selfish. So it made up its mind to go away from the house and never to come back.

It walked slowly to the door, groaning again under the weight of all its dishes. Mrs Snip and the tailor guessed what it was trying to do, and they rushed at it to push it back. The table rose up on two of its legs and began to punch with its other two.

Crash! Smash! Bang! Splosh! Every dish on the table slid off to the floor! There lay meat, pudding, pie, cakes, everything, and a whole heap of broken china. My, what a mess!

The table was pleased to be rid of its burden. It capered about and gave Mr Snip a punch on the nose. The tailor was frightened and angry. He really didn't know how to fight a fierce table like this. He tried to get hold of the two legs, but suddenly great claws shot out of the table's paws and scratched him on the hand.

Then the table slapped Mrs Snip and smacked Amelia and Paul hard. Then it squeezed itself out of the door and ran away down the street. It went on all-fours as soon as it left the house, and was so pleased with itself that it capered about in a very extraordinary way, making everyone run to their windows and doors in amazement.

Well, of course, the news went round that the marvellous magic table was loose in the land. Everyone secretly hoped to get it, and everyone was on the look-out for it. But the table was artful. It hid when the evening came and thought hard what it wanted to do.

"I will put myself into a museum," said the table to itself. "A museum is a place where all sorts of interesting and marvellous things are kept for people to wonder at and admire. I will find a museum and go there. Perhaps no one will notice that I have come, and I shall have peace for a while."

It wandered out into the street again, and went to the next town. It was a big one, and the table felt sure it would have a museum. It had – but the door was shut.

The table looked round the building to see if a window was open. Sure enough there was one, but rather high up. However, the table cared nothing for that. It climbed up a drainpipe with all its four paws, and squeezed itself in at the window. Then it clambered down the wall inside and looked about for somewhere to stand.

Not far away was a big four-poster bed, a square table, and two solid looking chairs. They had all belonged to some famous man. The table thought it might as well go and stand with these things, so off it went and arranged itself in front of the chairs. Then it went comfortably to sleep.

But in the morning it was, of course, discovered at once! The museum keeper saw it first, and perhaps he would not have known it was the lost magic table if the table had not suddenly scratched one of its legs with a paw, nearly making the poor man faint with amazement.

"It's the enchanted table!" he cried, and ran off to spread the news.

Soon the room was quite full of people, all staring and exclaiming, wondering

how in the world the table had got into their museum. Then of course began the rapping and the commanding of all kinds of food to appear. The table sighed. It was getting very tired of bearing the weight of so many heavy dishes. It was surprised to think that people seemed to be hungry so often.

It didn't like being in the museum after all. It was dreadfully cold; there was no fire there as there had been at the tailor's, and a terrible draught blew along the floor. The table shivered so much that all the dishes on it shook and shivered too.

That afternoon a message arrived from the King. He wanted the marvellous table in his palace. It would save him such a lot of money in feasts, he thought, and it would bring him a lot of fame.

The table heard the people talking to the messenger and it felt quite pleased. It would be warmer in the palace, at any rate. It got up and walked to the door. The people ran away as it came near, for they had heard how it had fought the tailor's family and defeated them.

But the table didn't want to fight. It just wanted to get somewhere nice and warm. The museum keeper tried to shut the door to stop it from going out, but the table pushed him over and went out, doing a jig to keep itself warm. It meant to walk to the palace.

Everyone thought that it was going to run away again, and men, women, and children followed it to see what it was going to do. They were filled with surprise to see it mounting the palace steps one by one, and entering the palace doors!

"It's gone to see the King!" they cried.

The table walked into the palace and no one tried to stop it, for all the footmen and soldiers were too surprised to move. The table went into the King's study, and found the King there, writing a letter.

"Who is it? Who is it?" asked His Majesty crossly, not looking up. "How many times have I said that people must knock before they interrupt me?"

The table went up to the King and bowed so low that it knocked its carved edge on the floor. Then it stood up and saluted with one of its paws.

The King looked up – then he sprang from his chair and ran to the other side of the room in a fright, for he had never seen a table like that before.

The table went over to the fire to warm itself. Soon the King recovered from his fright and called his servants.

"Here is that wonderful table," he said. "Take it to my dining-hall, and send out invitations to all the kings, queens, princes and princesses living near to

come and feast tonight. Tell them they shall each have what they like to eat and drink."

The table went into the gold-and-silver dining-hall, and thought it was very grand indeed, but cold. It pointed one of its paws at the empty grate, but as nobody imagined that a table could feel cold, no notice was taken at all. So the table contented itself with doing a little dance to warm itself whenever it began to shiver, and this amused all the servants very much.

When the time for the feast drew near, the footmen laid a wonderful golden cloth on the tabletop. Then they set out golden plates and dishes, golden spoons and forks, and golden-handled knives. How they glittered and shone!

No food was put out, not even bread. No, the table was to supply that.

Soon all the guests arrived, and how they stared to see such an empty table! "But there is nothing to eat!" whispered King Piff to Queen Puff.

"Take your seats," said the King, smiling. "I have brought you here to-night to see my new magic table, as enchanted and as bewitched as any table can be! Behold!"

He rapped smartly on the table three times. "A dish of crusty rolls! Some slices of new-made toast!" he cried.

Before his guests' wondering eyes these things appeared, and the King bowed a little as if he were a conjurer performing tricks.

"Now, Queen Puff," he said, "kindly say what you would like for your dinner, and I will see that it comes. Rap three times on the table before you speak."

Queen Puff did as she was told. "Celery soup, stewed shark's fin, roast chicken, roast beef, cauliflower, potatoes and plum pudding!" she said, all in one breath.

"Oh, and gingerbeer to drink!"

One by one all the guests wished for the dinner they wanted and marvelled to see everything appear on the table in an instant, all steaming hot and beautifully cooked. They sat and ate, lost in wonder. Then King Piff had an idea.

"I say," he said to the King who had invited him, "won't it give you – er – gold, for instance?"

Everybody there listened breathlessly, for one and all they loved gold, and wanted as much as they could get.

"Well," said the King, "I've never tried anything but food. Perhaps it would spoil the magic of the table if we did. We'd better not."

"Pooh! You mean to try when we're not here, so that you can get as much gold as you want for yourself!"

"Yes, you old miser!" cried Prince Bong, and everyone began to talk at once. The King was horrified to hear himself called such names, and he threatened to call in his soldiers and have everyone arrested.

No one listened to him. They were all rapping hard on the poor table, crying out such things as "A bag of gold! A sack of gold! Twenty diamonds! Six rubies! A box of jewels! Twenty sacks of gold! A hundred bars of gold!"

The poor table began to tremble. It had never been asked for such things

before, and had always been able to give what was demanded. But the magic in it was not strong enough for gold and jewels. It tried its best, but all it could give the excited people were sacks of cabbages, bags of apples, and bars of chocolate!

"Wicked table!" cried Prince Bong, and drew his sword to slash it.

"Horrible table!" cried Queen Puff, and slapped it hard. But that was too much for the frightened table. It jumped up on two legs and began to fight for itself.

Down slid all the dishes, glasses, plates and knives! The King found a roast chicken in his lap, and Queen Puff was splashed from head to foot with hot gravy. Prince Bong howled when a large ham fell on his toe, and altogether there was a fine to-do.

The table hit out. *Slap!* That was for the King. *Slosh!* That was for Prince Bong. *Punch!* That was for King Piff. *Scratch!* That was for Queen Puff. Oh, the table soon began to enjoy itself mightily!

But, oh my, the King was calling for his soldiers, and the table could not hope to fight against guns. It suddenly ran down the dining-hall, jumped right over the heads of the astonished soldiers, and

disappeared out of the door. How it ran!

"After it, after it!" yelled the King, who did not mean to lose the magic table if he could help it. But the table had vanished into the darkness.

It stumbled on and on, grieving that it could find no place where it would be treated properly. All it wanted was a room with a warm fire, a good polish once a week, and no kicking. At last it came to a funny-looking shop, lit inside by one dim lamp. The table peeped in. What a funny collection of things there was there! Old-fashioned furniture, suits of armour, rugs from far countries, lovely vases, old glasses, beaten-brass trays, strange, dusty pictures – oh, I couldn't tell you all there was.

It was a shop kept by an old man who sold strange things. Outside hung a sign on which was written the word ANTIQUES. The table did not know what that meant. All it knew was that there was a fire at the end of the shop, and that everything looked dusty and old – surely a table could hide here and never be discovered!

It crept in at the door. There was the old man, reading a book as old as himself, and the table hoped he would not look up as it walked softly among the dusty furniture.

"Who's there? Who's there?" said the old man, still not looking up. "Wait a minute – I must just finish my page, and I'll serve you."

The table squashed itself into a corner by the fire. It put up one of its paws and pulled down an embroidered cloth from the wall to cover itself. Then it heaved a sigh and stood quite still, enjoying the fire.

When the old man had finished his page he looked up – but there was no one in his shop. How strange!

"I felt sure I heard someone!" he said, rubbing his chin and looking all round, but he could see no one. So he went back to his book, and the table sidled a bit nearer the fire.

From that day to this no one has ever heard of that enchanted table. There it stands, happy and forgotten, in the old furniture shop, warming itself by the fire. If ever you see a round table with little animals carved round its edge, and with four big paws for feet, buy it. It is sure to be the long-lost enchanted table. But do be careful how you treat it, won't you?

Andrew's
Robin

In Andrew's garden there was a robin which he called his own. It was a black-eyed, long-legged, red-breasted little bird, so tame that it would take a bit of biscuit from Andrew's fingers.

That summer the robin had built its nest in an old saucepan under the hedge. Andrew remembered putting the saucepan there when he played house, and he had forgotten to take it away. The robin found it, and he and his little mate had put a cosy nest there.

Andrew was pleased. He watched the robins going to and from the nest. He saw the five eggs they laid there. He even saw three of the eggs hatch out. That was exciting. The tiny birds inside the eggs pecked at the shell and broke it.

Then out they came – bare black babies without a single feather on them.

The next day all five eggs had hatched. The robins threw the empty shells out of the saucepan nest and began hunting for caterpillars and grubs to feed their five hungry babies.

"That will keep you busy," said Andrew as he peeped at the five tiny birds, all with their beaks wide open. "When I dig my garden I will hunt for caterpillars too, and bring them to you."

One day a dreadful thing happened to the robins. A grey squirrel came that way and saw the nest in the saucepan. Now the grey squirrel liked, for a change, to make a meal of baby birds, so when he saw the little robins he ran over to them at once.

The father and mother robin were not there as they had gone hunting for grubs. The squirrel picked up two of the tiny creatures in his mouth and ran off with them.

How those babies squeaked! The father and mother robin heard them at once and came flying back. When they saw the grey squirrel they knew quite well what he had been up to and they flew at him, singing loudly in anger, for that is the way of robins.

The squirrel stopped. One robin flew at his right eye and the other flew at his left. He shook his head. He dodged. But it was no use. Those robins would not leave him alone until he dropped the baby birds.

So the grey squirrel dropped them on the lawn and then bounded off to a tree. Up he went and sat there making faces at the robins.

The robins flew down to their two frightened babies. They were not really hurt – but they could not possibly get back to the nest themselves.

"We must carry them in our beaks," sang the mother robin. But alas! The babies were too heavy.

"Leave them, leave them!" sang the freckled thrush. "I don't bother about my young ones if they fall from the nest."

But the robins were not like the thrush. They would not leave their little ones. But what could they do? The babies were too heavy to carry.

"Fetch Andrew, fetch Andrew!" sang the father robin. "He is kind and strong."

So the robins went to fetch Andrew. He was in his room, building a big castle, and was very surprised to see the two robins fly in at the window. The father robin flew to the top of Andrew's big castle and sang loudly to him. Andrew

stared at him. The robin flew to the window and back again.

"What is it you want?" asked Andrew, puzzled. The robin sang again and flew to the windowsill. Andrew got up and went too – and he saw something on the lawn. What could it be?

He ran downstairs and out into the garden. As soon as he came to the baby birds, lying helpless on the grass, he guessed why the robins had come to him.

"They want me to put their babies back," said Andrew in delight. "Oh, the clever little things! They knew I would help them."

He gently lifted the two frightened baby birds and took them to the nest in the saucepan. He put them with the others and they soon settled down happily.

"Thank you!" sang the robins. "You are kind!"

The robins were afraid of the squirrel

after that. Always one of them stayed to guard the nest until the babies were too big to be taken away by a squirrel. Soon they could fly. Soon they had flown. The little robin family split up and they all left the garden, except for the father robin. This little bird stayed there with Andrew, singing to him as he played in the garden. He never once forgot how kind the little boy had been to the baby birds.

One day Andrew took his clockwork train and railway lines on to the lawn. He set the train going and had a wonderful time with it. When it was teatime he had to pack it up in a hurry and go in, and it wasn't till the next day that he found he had lost the key of his beautiful clockwork engine.

"Oh, Mummy, now I can't play with my engine any more, because the key is lost," he said. "I have hunted everywhere in the garden, but I can't find it. I am so unhappy."

The robin heard him. He had seen Andrew winding up the engine. He guessed what the key was – that little

shiny thing. He began to hunt for it.

And at last he found it. No wonder Andrew couldn't see it, for it was halfway down a worm's burrow. The robin pulled it out. It was a bit rusty, but it was the lost key, no doubt about that.

The robin took it in his beak and flew to Andrew's playroom. He sat on the windowsill and made a little creamy sound, for he couldn't sing very loudly with something in his beak. Andrew looked up.

"Oh!" he cried in great delight. "You've found my key! You dear, good little bird! Thank you so much!"

"You helped me, and I helped you!" carolled the robin. "That is as it should be. Soon it will be wintertime, Andrew. Help me again and give me crumbs."

"I will, I will!" promised Andrew. And I know he will keep his promise.

Trundle Goes
Out to Tea

If ever you go to the little brownie village
of Tucked-Away you will notice a curious
thing. You will see that every brownie
wears a green leaf sewn onto his tight
little breeches, just over his right knee-
cap. And you are sure to wonder why.

Well, I will tell you the reason, because
I'm sure you won't like to ask the
brownies. We shall have to go right back
to the day when Trundle the brownie
went out to tea.

Now Trundle didn't live in the village
of Tucked-Away. Oh dear me no, he lived
in the town of Very-Big, where everything
was up-to-date, and all the brownies wore
the very latest thing in pointed caps, and
knew how many buttons should go on a
coat, and important things like that.

The brownies of Tucked-Away were very old-fashioned, although they tried hard not to be. As Trundle said, they simply did not know how to dress. They wore fifteen buttons down their coats when everyone in Very-Big was only wearing fourteen, and had five pockets instead of two.

The village of Tucked-Away thought a lot of Very-Big, and whenever a visitor from the town paid them a visit they were very excited. They made everything as nice as they could and tried their hardest to show the visitor that they could do things quite as well as Very-Big.

So you can imagine that when Trundle said he would go and have tea with his cousin in Tucked-Away there was great excitement. Trundle was a very up-to-date brownie, and always dressed just so. Jinks, his cousin, couldn't keep the news to himself when he got Trundle's letter, and he rushed round to all his friends to tell them that a brownie from Very-Big was coming to tea the very next Friday.

"I'll have a tea-party," he said, "and you must all come, dressed in your very best things, and we'll show Trundle that the village of Tucked-Away can be just as well dressed as the town of Very-Big!"

So everyone began to take out their best suits and sponge them and iron

them. They polished up the buttons and put clean handkerchiefs in the breast pockets, all ready for the tea-party.

Jinks made lots of scones and cakes and bought three different sorts of jam from the jam-woman. He made a yellow jelly and a red one, and when the day came you should have seen his tea-table. It was enough to make your mouth water! The brownies going by his cottage in the morning peeped in through the window, and what they saw made them long for the afternoon to come.

Jinks had asked everybody to come at four o'clock. Trundle was coming at half-past three, and Jinks thought that his visitor would just have time to wash and polish up his shoes before all the guests arrived.

At half-past two Trundle started out from the town of Very-Big to walk to Tucked-Away, which was four miles away. He had on his newest suit, and a fine new hat with a red feather in it. He liked his cousin Jinks and he was looking forward to the tea-party, for he hadn't had much lunch.

He went merrily along, whistling a

tune, walking in the shade, for the sun was hot. He was very nearly at Tucked-Away when a dreadful thing happened. Trundle caught his foot on a root and tumbled right over! And when he got up again, he found that he had torn a big hole in his nice red breeches, just over his right knee-cap!

"Oh, my!" said Trundle, in dismay. "Now isn't that unfortunate? Never mind, Jinks is sure to offer me a needle and thread when I get to his house, and I'll just have to mend it as best I can." He took a green leaf, and tucked it into the hole, for his knee was grazed and bleeding a little, and he didn't want his socks to be stained. Then he went on his way again, and soon arrived at Jinks's little cottage.

Jinks was at the door to greet him, and took him indoors to wash after his dusty walk. Jinks looked at his cousin's suit carefully, and decided that his own was just as fashionable – and then he caught sight of the green leaf stuck over Trundle's knee-cap.

"Dear me!" he thought. "That's a new idea, surely! I suppose it's a sort of trimming. Dear, dear, dear, and not one of my guests will be in fashion now, for none of us has got green-leaf trimming on his right knee! What can I do? There's half an hour before the tea-party begins, so perhaps there's just time to send little notes round and tell everyone to wear a green leaf sewn on to their right knee."

"The guests won't be here for a little while, Trundle," said Jinks to his visitor. "Would you like to go and sit out in the garden, and rest after your long walk?"

So while Trundle was resting in the garden, Jinks hurriedly wrote lots of little notes and gave them to his servant to deliver.

Please be sure to wear a green leaf as a trimming, sewn over your right knee-cap, said each note. *It is the latest fashion in Very-Big. Trundle is wearing one this afternoon.*

You can guess that when the guests received these notes they all rushed out in a great hurry, and got green leaves to

sew on to their right knee-caps. That took time, so they were all a bit late when they arrived.

Trundle fell fast asleep in the garden, and when he awoke he saw the first of the guests coming in at the gate.

"My goodness!" he cried. "I haven't mended this hole in the knee of my breeches! Whatever will the guests think of me?"

He got up to go and shake hands with the little brownie coming into the garden. When he saw the first one, he was very much astonished.

"What an extraordinary thing!" he thought. "Here's another brownie who must have tumbled down and torn his suit too, because he's got a green leaf over his knee-cap like me!"

His astonishment was even greater when he saw that the second brownie had a green leaf over his knee as well. And the third one, and the fourth! And his cousin, who certainly hadn't when he had met him at the door!

"Bless us, they've *all* got green leaves on their knees!" thought Trundle in the greatest amazement. "Am I in a dream, or what?"

He thought he really couldn't be, for the cakes tasted just like real ones, and as for the jelly, it was simply lovely. All the brownies seemed so very pleased with themselves, and looked proudly, first at Trundle's leaf-trimmed knee and then at their own.

Trundle was more and more puzzled, until a little brownie suddenly helped him to solve the mystery.

"Such a pretty new fashion, the leaf-trimming on the knee, isn't it?" said the brownie to Trundle. "As you see, Tucked-Away is not behind Very-Big in fashion!"

"Well!" thought Trundle. "Why in the world do they think that there's a fashion of that sort in Very-Big? There certainly isn't and never will be! I wonder – I wonder – is it possible that Jinks thought I was wearing this leaf as a sort of trimming and didn't guess I'd tumbled down and torn my breeches? He certainly didn't offer me a needle and thread to mend it with as I thought he would. I suppose he sent round notes to all the guests to tell them to wear leaves too, so as to be in the fashion! Oh, dear me, what a joke!"

Trundle had guessed quite rightly, and it made him smile to look round the tea-party and see everyone proudly wearing leaves over their right knees, thinking that they were very fashionable indeed.

"I mustn't let them know that there's no such fashion," he thought. "They would be so terribly upset – but, oh dear, if this isn't the very funniest thing that ever I saw!"

Trundle tried his hardest not to laugh, for he was a kind-hearted little brownie, but for once he was quite glad when the party came to an end. He wanted to laugh and laugh!

And all the way home he *did* laugh! You should just have heard him! Even the rabbits peeped out of their holes and laughed too, although they didn't know why!

From that day to this the village of Tucked-Away has kept to the fashion – so if ever you meet a brownie wearing a green leaf on his right knee, you will know where he comes from!

When the Donkey Sneezed

Neddy the donkey stood and looked at the cloudy sky. The sun had gone in a long time ago and the clouds were big and black.

Suddenly Neddy felt a sneeze coming. It was a great big sneeze, and he shut his eyes and opened his mouth.

"A-tish-ee-haw! A-tish-ee-haw!" he sneezed, very loudly indeed. That is the way that donkeys always sneeze, you know – a-tish-ee-haw! When the sneeze was finished, Neddy opened his eyes again – and just at that very moment a most enormous wind blew up! My goodness me, it was a wind! The clouds shot across the sky in no time, the trees went *wisha-wisha-wisha* all together, as their hundreds of leaves brushed one against the other, and the flag on the church tower waved like mad.

"Well, look at that!" said Neddy the donkey, astonished and proud. "That's what my sneeze has done – made this enormous wind! Would you believe it? I'm a very clever donkey, I am!"

Neddy didn't know that the wind had nothing at all to do with his sneeze. He really and truly thought that because he had sneezed such a big sneeze he had

made the wind come all by himself. He was as pleased as could be. He straightened up his ears, flicked his tail round, and galloped over to where the ducks were waddling off the pond.

The wind had made such big waves there that they were afraid and were hurrying off the water. Neddy brayed loudly and spoke to them.

"Hee-haw! Do you know, I sneezed just now and made the big wind come that is blowing waves on your pond?"

"Quack!" said all the ducks together. "Then we think you are very silly. Tell the wind to stop."

But Neddy didn't stop to listen. He ran off to the hens, who were all huddling under the hedge out of the gale.

"Hee-haw! Do you know, I sneezed just now and made the big wind come that is blowing all your feathers up the wrong way?"

"Cluck!" the biggest brown hen, said angrily. "What a silly thing to do! Tell the wind to stop!"

Neddy hee-hawed loudly, and laughed.

He was very proud of having made the wind come because of his big sneeze.

"No," he said, "I shan't make the wind stop. I think it is a grand wind."

"Cock-a-doodle-doo!" said a big cock, crossly. "You are stupid, Neddy. Look at my tail! It is almost blown off!"

But Neddy kicked up his heels and scampered away to the pigsty, where Mrs Sow and all her little pigs were crouching down in a corner, trying to keep out of the cold wind.

"Hee-haw! Do you know, I sneezed just now and made the big wind come that is blowing all the straw about in your sty?"

"Grunt!" said Mrs Sow, very annoyed. "Well, tell it to stop, you silly donkey! Nobody likes a wind like this."

"Oh, I shan't tell it to stop!" said Neddy. "It is my wind, and a very nice wind too. Ho ho, I'm a clever donkey, I am!"

Off he went again and galloped to the two brown horses that stood trying to shelter themselves under a tree. Their manes were blown upright in the wind and they shivered.

"Hee-haw! Do you know, I sneezed just now and made the big wind come that is blowing your manes about?" Neddy said proudly.

"What a silly thing to do on a cold day like this!" said the horses, neighing. "Who wants a wind at this time of year? Make it stop at once!"

"Not I!" laughed Neddy, and trotted away to Tibbles, the farmyard cat, who was hiding under a bush, very much

afraid of the stormy wind that was blowing her whiskers backwards.

"Hee-haw! Do you know, I sneezed just now and made the big wind come that is blowing your fur flat?" said Neddy, proudly.

"Well, that's nothing to be proud of!" Tibbles said crossly. "I was just drinking some milk out of my saucer on the kitchen step, and when the wind came it took hold of my saucer and tipped it up. Over went my milk and I lost my breakfast! Tell the wind to stop at once!"

"Not I!" laughed Neddy, pleased to

The Farmer Daily

think that so many things had happened because of his big sneeze. "Ha ha! What fun I am having!"

Well, all that day the wind blew, and what a nuisance it was! The flag blew right off the church tower, the big ash tree had a branch broken off, the pond was so rough that not even the biggest duck dared to swim on it, and it was really dangerous to cross the farmyard, because there were so many things blowing about in it. One little chick got quite lost in a big newspaper that suddenly blew over it, and its mother was very upset to hear it cheeping underneath. Altogether it was a dreadful day.

When teatime came all the farmyard animals met together and talked.

"Neddy the donkey must be made to stop this wind!" said one brown horse.

"We will tell him that if he doesn't sneeze again and stop it, we will pull his tail very hard indeed," said the biggest duck.

"Let's go and find him," said the cat.

So off they all went and found Neddy standing in the middle of the field, still feeling proud of his big wind, but shivering with cold.

"Neddy, you must stop this wind or we will all pull your tail hard," said Mrs Sow, grunting.

"I don't know how to stop it," said the donkey, rather frightened.

"Well, you started it with a sneeze, so I suppose you can stop it with a sneeze," said a cock. "We will all stand round you in a ring, and when we say 'Go!' you must sneeze. Now, are you ready?"

All the animals and birds stood in a ring round the donkey, and the cock said "One, two, three – GO!"

Then they all listened for Neddy to sneeze – but he couldn't! You simply can't sneeze on purpose, can you? – and no more could the donkey. He shut his eyes and opened his mouth ready for a good sneeze, but it wasn't a bit of good. It wouldn't come, and at last he shut his mouth and looked at the creatures round him.

"I can't sneeze, please," he said, in a very little voice.

"Nonsense!" said the cock. "If you don't, we shall pull your tail!" But still Neddy couldn't sneeze, so one by one all the animals and birds pulled his tail – and you should have heard him bray! He was so upset!

Whilst they were all doing this, the wind gradually dropped. Soon there was

none at all, and the trees stood quite still and quiet. Nobody noticed that the wind had gone and one by one all the animals and birds went home, leaving the poor donkey alone in the middle of his field.

"It serves me right for being so proud!" he thought. "But, dear me – look at this! The wind has gone! Now, what could have made it go? I didn't sneeze! Was it because I had my tail pulled that the wind stopped? Oh dear, if it was, I am afraid that all the animals will come and pull it again whenever they want the wind to stop. I couldn't bear that, so I will pack up my things and go far away where nobody knows about my sneeze."

So he packed up the few things he had and galloped right away. Where he went to nobody knows, but I expect he is very careful about his sneezing, don't you?

The Big Red Engine

Morris had a big red engine. It was made of strong wood, and was big enough to carry somebody if they sat on the boiler.

Morris liked to go to the top of the hill with his big red engine, sit on the boiler, and then let the engine carry him downhill at top speed. It really was fun.

But he wouldn't let anyone else do that. He didn't like sharing his toys. Some children don't – and, of course, nobody likes them much then.

Sometimes he went shopping for his mother, and then he put all the goods into his engine cab, taking them home like that, pulling on a piece of rope he tied to the funnel. That was fun.

"Please let me put my shopping into your engine cab," Molly said to him one day. "There's plenty of room. These potatoes are so heavy."

"No. My engine only carries my goods," said Morris.

"You're mean and selfish," said Molly. "Nobody likes you! One day you'll find your engine gone, and it will serve you right!"

"What do you mean?" Morris said in alarm. But Molly had gone, carrying her heavy bag of potatoes.

Now, the next week Morris did such a lot of shopping for his mother that she gave him some money to spend. He thought he would go and buy some sweets. Yes, he would buy some big humbugs – the black stripy ones that lasted a very long time.

He met James and Betty and Lennie. He showed them his money. "I'm going to buy a bag of humbugs," he said.

"Will you give me one?" asked little Betty.

"No. Why should I?" said Morris. "You've never given me a sweet, have you? Get out of my way, please. I'm going

66

downhill to the sweet-shop on my red engine. You watch me chuff down at top speed!"

The three children watched Morris get astride the boiler of the engine, put up his feet and then, hey presto, the engine rolled away down the hill to the sweet-shop. Morris shouted "Chuff-chuff-chuff" as he went. He felt rather proud.

He came to the sweet-shop. There was

a push-chair outside and a bicycle, too. There wasn't any room to park his engine. So he left it outside the shop next door. Then in he went to choose his sweets.

The shop had no humbugs that day. Morris looked round at all the jars and boxes. What should he have then? It really was difficult to choose. He thought about it for a long time and the shop assistant got impatient.

At last he chose some toffees, and the assistant weighed them out. Then she looked out of the window.

"My word! Look at the rain!" she said. "You had better wait till it stops, or you will get soaked."

So Morris stayed in the shop and waited till the rain stopped. It was a nice shop to wait in. He looked at every kind of sweet there was.

"The rain's stopped now," he said at last, and out he went to get his engine.

But it wasn't there! There was nothing outside either shop. The push-chair had gone, so had the bicycle. And so, most certainly, had his red engine.

"It's those horrid children!" he said. "Lennie, Betty and James. They've taken it! Just because I wouldn't share my sweets with them. I expect Molly told them to take it. She said I'd find it gone one day."

He saw Lennie, Betty and James coming out of a shop farther up the road – and yes, Molly was with them. They had taken it, they had hidden it! He raced after them, shouting.

"Where's my engine? What have you done with it? Where is it?"

The four children turned round at once, looking surprised. "We haven't got your engine," said Molly. "Don't shout at us like that."

"You have! I left it outside those shops down there, and when I came out it was gone. You've taken it, you know you have – just because I wouldn't share my sweets!"

"Don't be silly," said Molly. "We wouldn't do such a horrid thing as take your engine. Not that you don't deserve it! You do! Now go away – you're making Betty cry."

Well, Morris stamped and raged, but it wasn't a bit of good. Nobody told him anything about his red engine. "I'm going home," he shouted. "I shall tell Dad. I shall get you all punished! I'm very upset."

He stamped off home, crying now, because he loved his red engine and it was terrible to lose it so suddenly. The other children went the other way. Betty was crying, too, because Morris had scared her. Molly comforted her.

"He's just a horrid, selfish boy. You don't need to worry, Betty. It serves him right to lose his engine."

Now, just as they passed the sweet-shop, a woman came out of the shop next door – and she was carrying Morris's red engine! She set it down and then called to the four children.

"Does this belong to you, children? I found it outside my shop in the pouring rain, and it's such a lovely toy that I took it inside the shop out of the wet. But now I can't find out who it belongs to!"

"Oh! It's Morris's engine!" cried Molly. "He thought we'd taken it. He's awfully cross about it. I'd better take it home to him."

"No, don't," said James. "It will do him good to think it's lost. Let him be miserable."

"Well, he deserves to be, but I think even if he's horrid we needn't be," said Molly. "I know how glad I am when I get back something I've lost. Come on, let's take it to Morris."

So they all took it to Morris's house, taking turns to pull it along. Nobody felt like riding on the boiler. They came to Morris's house and went round to the back door.

Mr Felton, Morris's father, opened the door and exclaimed in surprise at the engine.

"Please," said Molly, "we've brought back the engine. The shop-lady next door to the sweet-shop took it into her place when it poured with rain, and then she couldn't find out who it belonged to. Morris left it outside her shop, you see. She told us all about it."

"I see," said Mr Felton. He called Morris. "Morris, come here. Your engine is back."

Morris came running. He pulled his engine indoors at once and glared fiercely at the four children.

"So you've brought it back, you horrid things! Where did you hide it? How dare you take my engine?"

"Morris," said his father, in a cold sort of voice, "somebody kindly took it into their shop out of the rain, and these four children found out by accident, and have brought it back for you. These are the children you have been saying horrid things about, and have refused to share your sweets with or so you told me. You said they had stolen your engine and didn't deserve a single sweet. What have you to say?"

Morris went scarlet. His mouth opened – but he hadn't a word to say.

"I think I'll give your engine to these four children," said Mr Felton. "And your sweets, too. I am surprised you can't even say you are sorry, or thank them for bringing it back. I'm ashamed of you."

He took the engine from Morris and pushed it towards Molly. But she shook her head.

"No, thank you," she said. "We don't want it. We don't want the sweets either. We only brought back the engine because we know how horrid it is to lose something you like. Goodbye, Morris."

The four of them went down the path. "I wouldn't like to have a boy like Morris if I was a dad!" said James.

"I wonder what his dad will say to him now," said Lennie. "I wonder if he'll let Morris keep his engine."

I don't know what Mr Felton did say to Morris – but I do know that he gives all the other children rides on his engine now, and takes Molly's shopping home in the cab, and shares every single bag of sweets all round. In fact, you wouldn't think that he was the same boy. So perhaps it was a very good thing that the shop lady took his red engine in out of the rain and made Morris think that he had lost it!

The Little Pig Who Squealed

There was once a toy pig in the play-room who had a most piercing squeal. "Eee!" he would squeal, "Eeeee!"

At first the toys thought it was funny. Not one of them had a voice as loud as the pig's squeal. But they soon grew tired of the squeal.

"Now stop it," they said to the toy pig. "There's nothing whatever to squeal about. Nobody should squeal unless something is the matter."

"When can I squeal then?" asked the pig. "When can I go 'Eee, eee, EEE!'"

"Don't do that," said the teddy bear, putting his paws to his ears. "You can only squeal when you are frightened of something, Pig. Then we'll come and rescue you."

"But don't squeal unless something is the matter!" said the toy mouse.

For two whole days the little pig didn't squeal. Nothing was the matter. Nothing frightened him. Well, there wasn't anything to be frightened of in the quiet playroom!

"My squeal will go if I don't use it," thought the little pig to himself. He tried it very softly. "Eeee. Oh, it's still there. It sounds funny if I squeal softly, though. I want to squeal loudly. But there's nothing the matter!"

Then he suddenly saw his own shadow behind him. He wasn't a bit frightened of it, but he pretended to be. "Eee, eeee, EEEE!" he squealed, and all the toys jumped in fright.

"What is it, what is it?" cried the teddy bear, running over to the pig.

"There is something dark and big behind me," said the little pig.

"It's only your own shadow!" said the teddy bear, looking. "Silly little pig! Don't squeal at your own shadow again!"

The pig had enjoyed his squeal. He

wanted to squeal again. It was fun to make the toys jump and come rushing over to him.

It began to rain the next day. The raindrops pattered on the window and the pig heard them. He knew quite well what they were but he thought he would squeal and pretend to be afraid. So he squealed.

"Eeee! Eeeeee!"

The little pig began to think it really was great fun to scare everyone when he squealed. He squealed for all kinds of things the next day!

"Eee-eee-EEE! I'm sure I heard the cat outside the playroom door!"

And every single time all the toys came running over to him, scared to hear him squeal. They were very cross when they found there was really nothing the matter. They told him off.

"What did we tell you, Pig? You are not to squeal unless something serious is the matter! You are very naughty."

The toys went back to their game. They were playing with the bricks out

of the brick-box and building a lovely little house for one of the small dolls.

"If that silly little pig squeals again I shan't take any notice," said the teddy bear, building a nice little front door.

"Nor shall I," said the toy mouse, looking for a brick that would do for a chimney. "He just squeals to make us jump."

"Well, let him squeal," said a big skittle, who was looking on. "He'll soon get tired of it if none of us pays any attention."

Now up on the big bookcase was a pile of books. The children had put them there ready to lend to someone who was ill. They hadn't piled them up very well, and every time a car went down the road the bookcase shook and the pile of books slid nearer and nearer to the edge of the shelf.

At last a lorry came by and the bookcase shook so much that the pile of books toppled over in a heap. Down they went, *crash-crash-crash*!

Nobody noticed that they had fallen on top of the little pig, who happened to

be on the floor just below. They covered him up completely.

He tried to squeal but he couldn't. He wriggled a little and moved one of the books. Then he could squeal.

How he squealed. You should have heard him! "EEEEE!" It was almost as loud as a toy train's whistle. It made the toys jump.

"That pig again!" said the teddy bear. "Screaming for nothing as usual, I suppose."

"Well, let him," said the skittle, looking round. "I can't see him anywhere. He's probably in the toy cupboard, pretending he's been shut in, and he's squealing for us to rush over and let him out."

"Well, we won't," said the teddy bear. "There, look – I've put on two chimneys. Don't they look fine?"

"EEEEE!" squealed the pig, under the pile of books.

"Squeal away," said the toy mouse. "We're tired of squeals that don't mean a thing. Now let me see – I think there are enough bricks left to build a wall."

"Eeeee," squealed the pig, but now his squeal wasn't quite so loud. A big book was pressing down so hard on his middle that it was spoiling his squeal.

"There he goes again," said the teddy bear. "I'm surprised he doesn't get tired of it when he knows we're not going rushing to find him!"

"Eeee-eee," squealed the pig, still more faintly. "Eeee."

"Ah, he'll soon stop," said the skittle. "I wonder where he is. If he's in the toy cupboard you'd think he would rattle at the door."

"Eeeee," said the pig, and now his squeal was so faint that it could hardly be heard. The big book had broken it.

"You know – I really think we ought to look for the pig," said the mouse, suddenly. "I mean – he doesn't usually squeal so softly. Perhaps there is something wrong."

So they all went to look for him – and there he was, buried under the books, feeling very sorry for himself indeed. Not a bit of his squeal was left!

"He's here – under the books!" said the bear. The toys dragged the books away and the little pig stood up unsteadily on his legs. "I squealed," he said, in a faint voice. "I squealed for help – and you didn't come."

"I know," said the teddy bear. "But it was your own fault, Pig. You squealed for nothing so often that we didn't know when you really were squealing for something. Still, no harm's done, as far as I can see. You're safe and sound – no bones broken!"

"Yes, but my squeal's broken," said the pig, sadly. "That big book pressed on it so hard that in the end it broke. I can't squeal any more. I've tried."

He tried again – but no squeal came, only a curious little sigh. The toys stared at him.

"Well," said the bear, "I never did like your squeal, Pig, and as you used it for the wrong things, it really does serve you right to lose it."

"I think the same," said the mouse. "But I'm sorry for you, Pig. You can come and live in the brick house we've built till you feel better about things. That will be a little treat for you."

So now the pig is living in the little brick house till he feels better. He doesn't know if his squeal will come back again or not – but if it does he'll be careful how he uses it!

The Girl Who Was
Left Behind

"Tomorrow we're going for a day by the sea, by the sea!" sang the children in Miss Williams's class.

"Well, mind you are none of you late for the coach," said Miss Williams, gathering up her books. "The coach will be at the Town Hall at ten o'clock. It will wait for ten minutes only, then it will start. So you must all be very punctual!"

"We'll be there before the bus!" said Millie.

"We'll be ten minutes early!" cried John.

"I'll have to do my mother's shopping first, but I can get there by ten o'clock," said Alice.

They all went home, happy because

they were to have a day's holiday by the sea tomorrow. Paddling, bathing, digging – what fun they would have!

All the children were up early the next day. It was Saturday. Most of them had little jobs to do. They had to make their own beds. They had to tidy up their toys. They had to feed chickens, or perhaps help with the shopping.

"I'm off to do my mother's shopping now," said Alice, peeping over the fence at Millie, who was sitting reading in her garden. "Wait for me, won't you? I'll be back as soon as I can. Then we'll run together to the Town Hall to get into the coach."

"I'll wait for you," promised Millie. "But don't be late, for goodness' sake!"

Alice set off. There was a lot of shopping to do, and the shops were full. She stood for a long time at the greengrocer's, but at last she was served. Then on she went to the baker's and to the chemist's.

She looked at a clock. Half past nine. She must hurry home now, because she had to put on a clean dress. She would just have enough time.

She hurried home. She gave her mother the shopping and counted out the change. She was a good, sensible little girl, and her mother trusted her with a lot of things.

Then she went upstairs to put on a clean dress. But, oh dear, it had a button missing! Never mind, there was just time to sew it on. Alice got out her needle and cotton.

Soon she heard Millie coming in from next door and calling up the stairs.

"Do come, Alice. It's five to ten! Do come. I shan't wait for you."

"Coming, coming!" cried Alice, and slipped her dress over her head. She buttoned it quickly, picked up her bag, and ran downstairs. She kissed her mother goodbye, and ran out with Millie.

"It's ten o'clock already," said Millie. "The coach will be there. We shan't get the best seats."

They ran down the street. Just as they got to the corner a boy came round on a bicycle. A dog ran across the road, and the front wheel of the bicycle ran into him. The dog yelped. The boy fell off his bicycle with a crash, and the bicycle fell on top of him. He lay still, stunned for a moment.

The girls stopped in alarm. Alice ran to

the boy. He opened his eyes and sat up, rubbing his knee, which was bruised and bleeding. "I feel funny," he said. "I've hurt my knee. Oh, look at my poor bicycle. I can't ride it home. The front wheel is bent. And all the things have fallen out of my bag. Could you pick them up for me, please?"

He was a boy about Alice's age, but she did not know him. She began to pick up the spilt things. Millie wouldn't help.

"Alice! We simply can't stop! Let someone else help him! We've got to catch that coach!"

"You help me, then, and we'll be able

to," said Alice. "You pick up the things, and I'll help the boy up. Go on, Millie."

"What, and miss the coach that is going to take us to the sea!" cried Millie. "It's five past ten already! I'm going. Are you coming or not, Alice?"

"Oh, yes, yes, just wait a minute. I can't leave this boy till he can stand up properly and wheel his bike," said Alice, anxiously. "There's nobody else about to help him. You go on, Millie, and just tell Miss Williams I'll be along in a minute. Don't let the coach go without me."

Millie ran off, looking cross. How silly of Alice to mess about like that! Let the boy help himself! He wasn't badly hurt. He could easily pick up his own things. Well, even if Alice was going to miss the coach, Millie wasn't!

She tore round the corner and ran down to the Town Hall. Thank goodness, the coach was still there. All the other children were in it. Miss Williams was standing beside it, looking anxiously for Millie and Alice.

"Where's Alice?" she said.

"Oh, she's messing about round the corner!" said Millie, unkindly. "She just won't be quick. I did tell her we'd be late. I left her behind."

"The naughty little girl," said Miss Williams, looking at her watch. "I'll wait one more minute, and then we shall go."

Alice helped the boy to his feet. He seemed a bit better. All his things were soon back in his bag. His bicycle could not be ridden so he would have to wheel it home.

"You sit down on that wall over there for a few minutes before you wheel your bike home," said Alice, "then you'll feel well enough. I'm sorry I can't stay and see you home, very sorry, but you see, the coach will only wait until ten minutes past ten."

She ran off and the boy looked after her, thinking what a kind little girl she was. It was nice to find someone kind

when you were hurt and dizzy. Kindness was one of the best things in the world.

Alice rushed round the corner and looked anxiously at the Town Hall, which she could see from there. There was no coach waiting for her! It had gone! Yes, there it was, climbing the hill beyond. It hadn't waited.

Alice stood and looked after it. It hadn't waited. Just because she had stopped to be kind, she had missed a lovely day by the sea. Millie, who hadn't been kind at all, had caught the coach.

"But I couldn't help stopping to help that boy," said Alice. "I just couldn't. And now the coach has gone without me."

Tears came to her eyes and trickled down her cheek. She had hurried so much, she had done all the shopping, she had had plenty of time to get to the coach – and yet she was left behind.

She turned to go home. She had forgotten about the boy sitting on the wall. She did not see him as she walked past him, her tears blinding her. She gave a little sob. She was so dreadfully, dreadfully, disappointed.

The boy saw her in surprise. Hadn't she told him she was going to catch a coach? Surely it hadn't gone without her!

"Hi!" he called. "What's the matter? Come over here and tell me."

So Alice told him, and then it was the boy's turn to comfort poor Alice. "What a shame!" he said. "I stopped you from catching the coach. Oh, I do feel dreadful about it. Poor, poor Alice."

"I can go home with you now, and wheel your bicycle, if you like," said Alice, wiping her eyes. "You look rather pale, and you ought to have your knee bathed. Come along."

So she took the boy home, wheeling his bicycle for him. He lived in a lovely house about three streets away. His mother was in the garden, and came running to meet him.

"What have you done, Donald? Oh, your poor knee. What has he done, what happened?"

Alice told her. Then Donald told his

mother how Alice had helped him. She was so grateful.

"Come along in and have some lemonade," she said. "I'll just bathe Donald's knee. I don't think it's really very bad."

While his mother was bathing his knee, Donald told her how poor Alice had missed the coach because she had stayed to help him. "So there will be no day by the sea for her," he said. "And all because of me!"

His mother looked thoughtful. Then she smiled. "Alice shan't miss her day by the sea!" she said. "I will take her, and you, too, in the car! It will do you good to have a blow by the sea, after this nasty little fall. We will go to your Auntie Lou's for the day and have a lovely time! Would you like that?"

"Oh, yes!" said Donald, cheering up at once. "Shall I go and tell Alice? Have you finished with my knee? Oh, won't she be pleased!"

Alice was. She could hardly believe her ears. After her big disappointment it seemed too good to be true that she was going to have a day by the sea after all! She thanked Donald's mother shyly, and her eyes shone with joy.

They soon set off in Donald's mother's little car. First they went round to Alice's mother and told her. She was very surprised, but pleased to know that Alice had been so kind.

Then off they went. It was a fast little sports car, and Donald's mother drove well. Alice enjoyed it. She had never been in a sports car before, and she thought it was lovely.

"We're going so fast," she said. "Do

you think we'll pass the coach that the others are in?"

"Well – they had a good start," said Donald's mother. "We may get there about the same time."

The funny thing was, they did! Just as the car drew up on the seafront for the two children to look at the calm blue sea, a big coach drew up too – and it was the one with all the schoolchildren in!

"Look! There's Alice! Surely that's Alice!" Millie cried in amazement. "Alice, Alice, how did you get here? We left you behind!"

She jumped down and ran to Alice. But Donald did not welcome her. "This is the other girl who saw me fall," he said to his mother. "But she didn't help. She just stood and said they would miss the coach, and ran off without Alice and she didn't even get the coach to wait!"

Millie went red. She knew she had been selfish and unkind. She went back to the others, still red. Now she wished she had been kind, too! Here was Alice, going to have a lovely day with Donald's nice mother – and going back in a sports car! And Millie had thought her so silly to stay behind and help.

Alice had a wonderful day. Donald's Auntie Lou was as kind as his mother, and they all four had a picnic on the beach and ice creams afterwards. They had ice creams again at teatime, and Donald and Alice had three rides each on a donkey, and a lovely bathe.

"Now we must go home," said Donald's mother, who had been watching Alice and thinking what a well-mannered, nice little girl she was. "Come along."

"Oh, I wish the day wasn't over!" said Alice with a sigh. "I have so loved it."

"We'll have more days like this," said Donald's mother. "You must come to tea with Donald every week. You will be a nice friend for him – someone who is kind and unselfish. Donald is kind, too, so you will make a good pair!"

They do, and they are very happy playing together. "Your bit of kindness brought you a big reward," Alice's mother said. It certainly did, but I think Alice deserved it, don't you?

The Clown's
Little Trick

In John's playroom were all kinds of toys, from the big rocking-horse down to the tiny clockwork mouse. They lived together happily and were kind and good to one another, just as John was kind to them.

But one day the fat little toy elephant wasn't so good after all. John had some little chocolate sweets and he seemed to enjoy eating them very much. The toy elephant watched him and wished he could taste one. "Don't eat any more, John," said his mother. "You must make them last all the week – three a day, I should think."

John put them away on the bottom shelf of his little bookcase. The toy elephant saw exactly where he put them.

And that night, in the dark, he left the toy cupboard, walked across the wooden floor and over the rug, to the little bookcase. He felt about with his trunk and found the paper bag.

He put his trunk inside and felt the little chocolates there. He got hold of one with his trunk and popped it into his mouth.

"My – it's good!" he whispered to himself. "Very, very good. I like it. Tomorrow night I'll fetch another."

He went back to the toy cupboard, stood himself in a corner and finished eating the sweet. All night long he tasted the flavour of it, and was happy. He didn't think how naughty he had been to take it.

The next night he did the same, putting his little trunk into the bag and pulling out a sweet. He ate it, and then he took another. Nobody saw him. He just stood there in the dark and enjoyed himself.

But John soon found that someone was taking his sweets. He looked sternly at his toys.

"Toys," he said, "it's very sad, but one of you is taking my sweets at night. Don't do it. It's very, very wrong."

The toys were dreadfully upset. They looked at one another when John had gone out for a walk.

"Can one of us be so horrid?" they said. "Who is it? He should own up at once!"

But the fat little elephant said nothing. He didn't even go red. He wasn't a bit ashamed of himself. And that night he crept off to the paper bag and took two more sweets! He really did.

John was very sad the next day. He looked at the teddy bear, the clockwork mouse, the clown, the monkey, the elephant, the pink cat, the black dog and all the rest of them.

"If it happens again I am afraid I shall have to lock the toy-cupboard door, so that none of you can get out at night," he said.

This was a horrid threat. The toys did so love to get out of the cupboard and play around sometimes when John was in bed. When the moon shone in at the window they often had a dance. It would be dreadful if John really did lock the cupboard.

When John had gone out of the room the clown stood up. "We simply must find out who is the thief," he said. "I am not going to let us all be punished for something that only one of us does! Let that one own up now before it is too late. For I warn him, I shall find him out."

The toy elephant didn't say a word. The clown frowned. "Very well," he said. "It will be very, very bad for the thief when I find him out."

Now, that night the clown did a funny thing. He crept into the larder and found the pot of honey there. He dipped in a paintbrush and hurried back to the playroom again. He carefully painted the bit of shiny floor outside the toy cupboard with the honey on the brush. It made it very sticky indeed.

Then the clown went to the bread-board in the kitchen and collected all the crumbs he found there. He took them to the little bookcase and scattered them just in front of the place where the paper sweet-bag was kept.

Then he hurried back to the toy cupboard and sat down beside the teddy bear. He didn't tell anyone at all what he had done.

The toys were tired that night. John had played with them a lot that day. They fell asleep and slept soundly, all but the fat little elephant who was waiting to go and get another sweet. When he was sure everyone was asleep, he crept out of the cupboard as usual. His four feet stepped on the honey. Then, with sticky feet, he padded over to the bookcase and put out his trunk to the sweet-bag.

He trod on the scattered crumbs. They stuck to his feet, but he didn't know it. He took a sweet and padded back to the toy cupboard. He spent a long time enjoying the little chocolate.

Now, just at dawn, when a silvery light

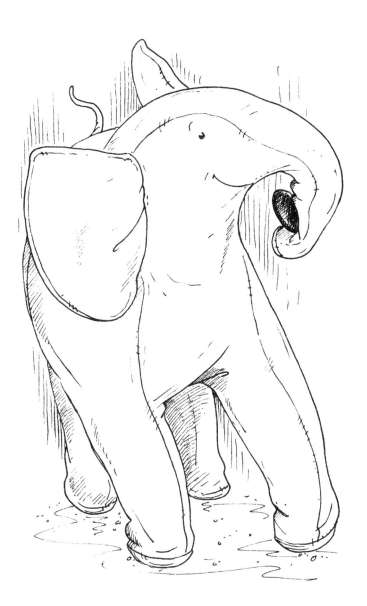

was coming in through the window, the clown woke all the toys up.

"Wake up," he said, and his voice sounded so stern that the toys were alarmed.

"What's the matter?" they said.

"I am going to show you who the thief is," said the clown. "I myself don't know who it is yet, but I soon shall know! Everyone sit down, please, and show me the soles of your feet!"

In great surprise all the toys did as they were told, and the clown looked at their feet quickly. And, of course, when he came to the elephant's feet, he saw the little crumbs sticking there, and smelled the honey on them, too!

"Here is the thief!" he cried. "Bad little elephant! Look, toys, he has crumbs stuck to his feet! You see, I spread honey just outside the cupboard, and scattered crumbs in front of the bookcase! And the elephant walked over the honey and the crumbs stuck to his feet! So now we know who the thief is! Bad little elephant!"

The toys were angry with the elephant. They turned him out of the toy cupboard. They made him go and stand in front of the sweet-bag, so that John would know who the thief was, when he came in.

And he did, of course. "So you were the bad little thief!" he said. "I'm ashamed of you. I won't play with you any more!"

And the fat little elephant cried tears into the brick-box at the back of the toy cupboard, and made quite a puddle there.

"Serves you right," said the clown. "We shan't play with you either for a night or two. Perhaps you will think twice the next time you want to take things that don't belong to you!"

It was a clever trick of the clown's, wasn't it?

A Coat for
the Snowman

Old Mrs White looked out of her bedroom window and frowned. "Snow!" she said. "Snow – thick and white and deep! How annoying. What a lot must have fallen in the night."

"Oh, look at the lovely snow!" shouted the children in the field nearby. "It's as high as our knees. Let's build a snowman."

"Silly children to play with the cold snow like that," said Mrs White, who wasn't very fond of children. "Now I suppose they will play in the field all day and make a terrible noise. Bother them all."

Micky, Katie, Olivia, Peter and Will played together in the snowy field that day and had a lovely time. They made their snowman. He was a real beauty.

He had a big round head, with twigs sticking out for hair. He had eyes of stones and a big white stone for a nose. He had a stone mouth, too.

He had a big fat body, and the children patted it all round to make it smooth. He looked very real.

"We must dress him," said Micky. "We want a hat for him." He found an old hat in a ditch. It just fitted the snowman nicely. He wore it a little to one side and looked very knowing indeed.

"We want a scarf, too," said Katie. "My aunt lives in that cottage nearby. I'll see if she has one."

She had. It was an old red one, rather holey, but it went round the snowman's neck quite well.

"He'll feel warm with this scarf," said Olivia. "It must be so cold to be made of snow. I do wish we had a coat for him to wear."

"Oooh yes – then we could fill the sleeves with snow and that would make him look awfully real," said Katie. "I'll ask my aunt for an old coat."

But her aunt said no, she hadn't a coat old enough for a snowman.

"Where can we get one?" asked Katie. "Shall I ask the old lady next door to you? What's her name? Mrs White?"

"Oh, you won't get anything out of her," said her aunt. "She doesn't like children. She's a grumbly old thing. You leave her alone."

"She looks very poor," said Olivia. "Hasn't she got much money?"

"Hardly any," said Katie's aunt. "Don't you go bothering her, now – she'll box your ears if you do."

The children went back to their snowman. They looked at him. It would be so very, very nice if he had a coat. He would be the finest snowman in the world then.

Just then old Mrs White, in big rubber boots, came grumbling out to get herself a scuttleful of coal. Micky saw her.

"Poor old thing," he said. "I'll get the coal for her." He hopped over the fence and went down the snowy garden. Old Mrs White saw him and frowned.

"Now, what are you doing coming into my garden without asking?" she scolded.

"I'll get your coal in for you," said Micky. "Give me that shovel."

He shovelled until the scuttle was full. Then he carried it indoors for Mrs White.

"That's kind of you," she said. "But I

hope you're not expecting money for that.
I've none to spare."

"Oh no, of course not," said Micky,
quite shocked. "My mother won't let me
take money for helping people. She says
you are not really helping if you're paid.
I don't want any reward at all, thank
you, Mrs White."

"Well now, I wish I could give you
something, that I do," said Mrs White,
feeling pleased with the little boy. "But

I've no biscuits and no sweets. You just look round my kitchen and tell me if there's anything you'd like. What about that little china dog?"

"I don't want anything, thank you," said Micky, looking round. He suddenly saw an old, old coat hanging up behind the kitchen door.

"Well," he said, "there's just one thing – do you think you could possibly lend us that old coat for our snowman, Mrs White? Only just *lend* it to us. We'll bring it back safely."

"Why, yes, if you want it," said old Mrs White. "It's a dirty, ragged old thing. I haven't worn it for years. I keep meaning to give it away. Yes, you take it. I shan't even want it back."

"Oh, thank you," said Micky. "Our snowman will look wonderful."

He unhooked the old coat from the door and ran back to the others with it. "Look what I've got!" he called. "Mrs White's given it to me for our snowman. Won't he look great?"

The children filled the sleeves with

snow and then hung the coat round the snowman. He certainly did look real now. There he stood in his old hat, scarf and coat, looking very smart.

"How do you do, Mr Shivers?" said Micky, walking up to the snowman and holding out his hand. "I hope you like this cold weather."

The others roared with laughter. The people passing by looked over the hedge at the snowman and called out that he was the best one they had seen. The children really felt very proud of him.

They left him standing there alone when it grew dark. But the next day they were back again. Alas, the snow had begun to melt, and Mr Shivers was a peculiar sight. He had slumped down, and all the snow had trickled out of his sleeves.

"He's going," said Micky. "I'll take Katie's aunt's old scarf back to her."

"We don't need to take Mrs White's coat back. She said we could keep it," said Peter. "Still, perhaps we'd better."

Micky jerked the coat off the melting snowman. He ripped the lining a little and some paper fell out.

"I say, what's this?" said Micky in surprise. "Why, it's money. There's fifty pounds! It must have slipped out of the pocket into the lining, and old Mrs White didn't know it was there. Gracious, let's go and give it to her."

They all tore off to Mrs White's cottage. She could hardly believe her eyes when she saw the money. "Why, now, I lost that money years and years ago," she said. "And proper upset I was about it, too. Thought I'd dropped it in the street, and all the time it was in my coat-lining. What a bit of good luck for me."

"Yes," said Katie. "I'm so glad."

"Bless your heart! What nice children you are. Maybe I've been wrong about boys and girls," said old Mrs White.

"Well, well, now I can buy myself a new cardigan and a new pair of shoes for my poor old feet."

She bought something else, too. She bought the biggest chocolate cake she could buy; she bought crisps and biscuits, a pound of mixed chocolates, five big balloons and a big box of crackers. And she gave a party for Micky, Katie, Olivia, Peter and Will.

They loved it. But in the middle of it Micky gave her quite a shock. "There's somebody who ought to have come to this party and isn't here," he said solemnly. "What a pity."

"Oh dear me, who's that?" said Mrs White, quite alarmed. "I am sorry I've forgotten one of you. Go and fetch him at once."

"We can't," said Micky, and he laughed. "It's Mr Shivers, the snowman, Mrs White. He ought to be the guest of honour, for without him we'd never have borrowed your coat and we wouldn't have found the money. What a pity old Mr Shivers isn't here."

The Cat
Without Whiskers

Inky was a black cat, with the finest white whiskers in the street. He was a handsome cat, with sharp ears and a long thick tail that looked like a snake when he waved it to and fro. He had a white mark under his chin which the children called his bib, and he washed it three times a day, so that it was always like snow.

Inky was plump, for he was the best ratter and mouser in the town, and never lacked a good dinner. When he sat on the wall washing himself he was a fine sight, for his glossy fur gleamed in the sun and his whiskers stuck out each side of his face like white wires.

"I'm the finest-looking cat in the town," said Inky proudly, and he looked scornfully down at the tabby in the garden below, and the white cat washing itself on a windowsill near by. "Nobody is as good-looking as me!"

Then a little boy came by, and when he saw the big black cat sitting up on the wall, he shouted up at him, laughing, "Hello, Whiskers!"

Inky was offended. His name wasn't Whiskers. It was Inky. A little girl heard what the boy said and she laughed. "That's a good name for him," she said.

"He's a very whiskery cat. Whiskers!"

Everyone thought it a funny name, and soon Inky was being called Whiskers all day long, even by the cats and dogs around. This made him really very angry.

"It's a horrid, silly name," he thought crossly, "and it's rude of people to call me that. They don't call that nice old gentleman with the beard 'Whiskers', do they? And they don't shout 'Nosy' at that boy with the big nose. I shan't answer them when they call me Whiskers!"

So he didn't – but it wasn't any good, for everyone shouted "Whiskers! Whiskers!" as soon as they saw Inky's wonderful whiskers.

Inky thought hard. "I shall get rid of my whiskers," he said to himself. "Yes – I shall start a new fashion for cats. We won't have whiskers. After all, men shave every morning, and people think that is a good idea. I will shave my whiskers off, and then no one will call me Whiskers."

He told his idea to wise old Shellyback the tortoise. Shellyback listened and pulled at the grass he was eating.

"It is best not to meddle with things you have been given," he said. "You will be sorry."

"No, I shan't," said Inky. "My whiskers are no use to me that I can see – I shall shave them off!"

Well, he slipped into the bathroom at his home early the next morning and found the thing his master called a razor. In an instant Inky had shaved off his beautiful whiskers. They were gone. He

was no longer a whiskery cat.

He looked at himself in the glass. He did look a bit strange – but at any rate no one would now shout "Whiskers" after him. He slipped down the stairs and out into the garden. He jumped on the wall in the sun.

The milkman came by and looked at him. He did not shout "Whiskers!" as he usually did. He stared in rather a puzzled way and said nothing at all. Then a young boy came by delivering papers, and he didn't shout "Whiskers!" either.

Inky was pleased. At last he had got rid of his horrid name. He sat in the sun, purring, and soon his friends gathered round him. There was Tabby from next door, the white cat Snowball, Shellyback the tortoise, who looked up at him from the lawn, and the old dog Rover, who never chased cats.

"What's the matter with you this morning, Inky?" asked Snowball, puzzled. "You look different."

"His whiskers are gone," said Tabby, startled. "How strange."

"How did you lose them?" asked Rover.

"I shaved them off," Inky said proudly. "I am starting a new fashion for cats. Grown-up men shave their whiskers off each day, don't they? Well, why should cats have whiskers? Don't you think I look much smarter now?"

Everyone stared at Inky, but nobody said a word. They all thought Inky looked dreadful without his whiskers.

"You'll soon see everyone following my fashion of no whiskers," said Inky. "It's much more comfortable. Whiskers always get in my way when I'm washing my face, but now I can wash it as smoothly as anything. Look!" He washed his face with his paw. Certainly it looked easier to do it without whiskers. But the older animals shook their heads.

"Whiskers must be some use or we wouldn't have them," said Tabby.

"Well, what use are they?" said Inky.

But nobody was clever enough to think of anything to say in answer to that. One by one they slipped off to their homes to dinner, quite determined that they were not going to shave off their whiskers, whatever Inky did.

Now that night Inky felt very hungry. He had been late for tea that afternoon and a stray dog had gone into his garden and eaten up the plate of fish and milk that his mistress had put out for him. Inky was annoyed.

"Never mind," he thought to himself. "I'll go hunting tonight. I'll catch a few mice and perhaps a rat or two. I know a good place in the hedge at the bottom of the garden. I'll hide on one side of it and wait for the night animals to come out."

So off he went when darkness came and crouched down on one side of the hedge. Soon he heard the pitter-pattering of little mice-feet. Inky stiffened and kept quite still. In a moment he would squeeze through the hedge and pounce on those foolish mice.

He took a step forward. His paw was like velvet and made no noise. He pushed his head into a hole in the hedge – then his body – but alas for Inky! His body was too big for the hole, and the hedge

creaked as he tried to get through. The mice heard the noise and shot off into their holes. Not one was left.

"Bother!" said Inky crossly. "I'll wait again. I believe that old rat has a run here somewhere. I'd like to catch him!"

So he waited – and sure enough the big rat ran silently by the hedge. Inky heard him and began to creep towards him; but his fat body brushed against some leaves and the rat heard and fled.

Inky was astonished. Usually he could hunt marvellously without making a single sound. Why was it that his body seemed so clumsy tonight? Why did he brush against things and make rustling noises? It was most annoying.

And then suddenly he knew the reason why. Although he hadn't thought about it, his fine whiskers had always helped him to hunt. They had stretched out each side of his face, and were just about the width of his body. He had known that if he could get his head and whiskers through a hole without touching anything, his body would go through easily too, without a sound.

"It was my whiskers that helped my body to know if it could go easily and silently through the holes and between leaves," thought Inky in despair. "Of course! Why didn't I think of that before? They were just the right width for my body, and I knew quite well if I touched anything with my whiskers that my body would also touch it and make a noise – and so I would go another way!"

Inky was quite right. His whiskers had helped him in his hunting. Now he would not be able to hunt well, for he would never know if his body could squeeze through gaps and holes. He would always be making rustling, crackling noises with

133

leaves and twigs. He would never catch anything. Poor Inky!

You can guess that Inky was always waiting for his mistress to put out his dinner after that – for he hardly ever caught a mouse or rat now. He grew much thinner, and he hid himself away, for he was ashamed to think that he had shaved off the things that had been so useful to him.

"A new fashion indeed!" thought Inky. "I was mad! If only I had my lovely whiskers again I wouldn't mind being called "Whiskers" a hundred times a day. My life is spoilt. I shall never be able to hunt again."

He was a sad and unhappy cat, ashamed to talk to anyone except wise old Shellyback the tortoise. One day he told Shellyback why he was unhappy. Shellyback looked at him closely and laughed.

"Go and sit up on the wall in the sun and see what happens," he said to Inky. "You'll find your troubles are not so big as you thought they were."

In surprise Inky jumped up on the wall and sat there in the sun. The milkman came by with his cart. He looked up.

"Hello, Whiskers!" he shouted. "Good old Whiskers!"

Inky nearly fell off the wall in astonishment. What! He was called Whiskers again even if he had shaved them off? But silly old Inky had quite forgotten something. What had he forgotten?

He had forgotten that whiskers grow again like hair. His whiskers had grown out fine and long and strong and white – and he had been so miserable that he hadn't even noticed. Silly old Whiskers!

He was happy when he found that he had them again. He sat and purred so loudly that Shellyback really thought there was an aeroplane flying somewhere near! It sounded just like it.

And now Inky can hunt again, and is the best mouser in the town. He has grown plump and handsome, and his whiskers are finer than ever. He loves to hear himself called Whiskers now. So if you see him up on the wall, black and shining, don't say "Hello, Inky!" – shout "Good old Whiskers!" and he'll purr like a kettle on the boil!

The Two
Cross Boys

Tom and Willie were cousins. Sometimes they went to stay with one another, and that was fun – at least, it would have been fun if they hadn't quarrelled so much!

The worst of it was that when they quarrelled they wouldn't make it up, and, of course, that's very silly. But Tom's mother cured them, as you will see.

Willie went to stay with Tom, and for the first two days they had a good time. Tom was so pleased to have Willie to play with that he let him have all his toys.

"You can ride my bicycle if you like!" he said. "You can use my skateboard when you want to. You can climb that tree down there in the garden that I call my very own."

"Thank you, Tom," said Willie, and he rode the bicycle, used the skateboard, and climbed the tree.

And then, after two days, they quarrelled. Quarrels are often about silly little things that don't really matter at all, and this one was so silly that you will hardly believe it.

Tom hit his elbow hard against the wall and it hurt him. The tears came into his eyes. Willie saw what he had done and he laughed.

"You shouldn't cry, Tom," he said, "you should laugh! That was your funny-bone you hit against the wall."

"It was not a funny bone at all," said Tom, who didn't know that we call the point of our elbow our funny-bone. "It wasn't a bit funny. It was horrid. I'm hurt."

"Well, if you won't laugh at your funny-bone, I shall!" said Willie teasingly. "Ha ha ha! Ho ho ho!"

"You horrid thing!" said Tom angrily. "You shouldn't laugh when people are hurt. I shan't speak to you!"

"Funnier than ever," said Willie. "Ha ha ha! Ho ho ho!"

Tom slapped him. Willie slapped back. Then they both yelled at the tops of their voices, for Tom had slapped Willie on the cheek and Willie had slapped Tom on the nose, and both places hurt.

Tom's mother came hurrying out. "Now, now," she said, "quarrelling again! I did think that this time you were old enough to play nicely together. Now, make up your quarrel, and then go and play football in the field, for a treat."

"I don't want to," said Tom, and he turned away.

"I shall never speak to Tom again," said Willie, as Tom marched off with his hands in his pockets, and his nose looking quite red from the slap it had received.

Tom's mother went indoors again, thinking what little sillies the two boys were. "I expect they'll soon get over it," she thought.

But, you know, they didn't! They wouldn't smile at one another or speak to each other all day. They wouldn't say

goodnight at night. They wouldn't sit next to each other at breakfast-time the next morning. It was very unpleasant for Tom's mother, for she did like smiling faces and happy talk.

"What are you going to do this morning?" she asked.

"Well, if Tom's going to be in the garden I shall be indoors," said Willie sulkily.

"And if Willie's in the house I shall be outside," said Tom at once.

"You are both very silly, stupid boys," said Tom's mother. "You are wasting all the time you have together just because you can't make up a quarrel about Tom's funny-bone."

"I'll do any jobs for you, Auntie," said Willie, feeling a bit ashamed of himself. "Give me some work to do and you'll soon see I'm not stupid."

"If anybody's going to do a job for my mother, I'm going to do it!" said Tom at once.

"Well, you shall both do a job for me," said Tom's mother, and she smiled a

141

funny little secret smile to herself.

"What is the job?" asked Tom.

"I want the big kitchen window cleaned," said Tom's mother.

"Well, Mum, I said if Willie's in the house I shall be out-of-doors," said Tom. "I won't work in the same place with him."

"Very well," said his mother. "Tom, you shall clean the inside of the window and Willie shall clean the outside. I've got two window cloths, so that will be all right."

In a little while the boys went to do their job. Each had a window cloth and some cleaner. Tom was to do the inside, and Willie was to do the outside of the window. Each of them was quite determined to do his side better than the other.

They began. They wouldn't look at one another, but Tom thought it would be fun to pretend to rub out Willie's red face. So he rubbed hard with his cloth just where Willie's face was. And then Willie guessed what he was doing, and he

decided he would rub out Tom's face!

So he ducked down to see Tom's face, and then began to try to rub him out through the glass!

Now you can't do things like this without feeling rather giggly. It's funny to begin with, to rub away so near to one another, with only the window in between – and it's funnier still if you are cross and try to rub someone out!

Then the boys found that their hands were rubbing in time, together – forward, back, one, two; forward, back, one, two!

Then they rubbed fiercely at one another's hands – and then they caught one another's eye, and found that each had a little twinkle in it!

"I shan't look at him," thought Tom. "If I do I know I shall laugh."

"I won't even peep at him!" said Willie to himself. "I feel as if I shall giggle if I do!"

But they did keep looking at one another just to see if the other was smiling – and soon Tom's mouth curled itself upwards, and he had to hide it in his handkerchief. Then Willie felt as if he was going to giggle, swallowed the giggle and choked and spluttered till he was scarlet in the face!

He looked so funny that Tom began to giggle too. He tried to stop. He shut his mouth. Another giggle burst out of it. He ran away to a corner of the room, put his head into a cushion and laughed till the tears came out of his eyes and trickled down the cushions.

Willie peeped through the window and saw what Tom was doing, and that made him laugh too. He sat on the window-sill and roared with laughter.

Tom's mother heard them and looked into the room. "Whatever are you laughing at, Tom?" she asked.

"Oh, Mum, it's so funny to clean a window with somebody else cleaning it outside," said Tom. "I just can't help laughing."

Tom's mother went outside. "What are you laughing at, Willie?" she said.

"Oh, Auntie, you should have seen Tom and me cleaning this window together!" he giggled. "Tom tried to rub me out and I tried to rub him out – it was so funny."

"Show me how funny it was," said Mother, and she called Tom. Then the two boys showed her, giggling as they rubbed their cloths to and fro across the window, grinning at one another.

Mother laughed and laughed. "Yes, it's very funny," she said. "Now would you both like to run down to the shop and buy yourselves an ice cream each for doing my window so nicely?"

Now you can't go on quarrelling with somebody you've giggled with. Every time Tom looked at Willie he laughed, and Willie kept giggling too.

"Yes, we'll go together," said Tom. "Come on, Willie. Let's be friends again. I can't laugh with an enemy!"

"Nor can I!" said Willie. So they were friends again. Mother gave them a pound and they went off to buy their ice creams. On the way Willie was rather thoughtful.

"What's the matter?" asked Tom.

"I'm just thinking about Auntie," said Willie. "She's really very clever, Tom. She knew we would laugh over cleaning the same window – she knew we would try to rub each other out. It was her way of making us friends! Didn't I giggle too! I nearly choked with trying not to!"

Wasn't it a good idea that Tom's mother had? Now when the boys quarrel she looks at them and says, "Do you remember how you cleaned that window together?" Then they giggle, of course, and everything is all right again!

The Little
Chocolate Man

When Eileen went to the Sunday School party, there was a huge Christmas tree there. All the children had presents from the tree, and Eileen was very pleased with hers. It was a little fat man made of chocolate, and he carried a thick walking stick of chocolate too.

So you see, he was a very grand chocolate man. He thought a lot of himself. He turned up his nose at the chocolate rabbits and laughed out loud at a little motor-car hanging near him on the tree.

"I'm a real slap-up right-to-the-minute chocolate man!" he said, though he didn't know what it meant. He had heard the shopkeeper say that when he had been sold to the Sunday School teacher who bought all the Christmas-tree toys. So he kept saying it to himself, feeling grander and grander every time he said it! When Eileen took him home she stood him on a shelf with her monkey, her soldier-boy and her Dutch doll. He was

pleased to be where he could look all round the room and see what was going on. He took a look at the toys beside him on the shelf and decided that he was much grander than they were. Ho, they were only stuffed toys, but he was made of chocolate!

"I'm a real slap-up right-to-the-minute chocolate man!" he said out loud.

"Dear me!" said the Dutch doll in a woodeny voice. "What a lot you think of yourself, to be sure!"

"Speak when you're spoken to," said the chocolate man rudely.

"Well, I thought I was spoken to!" said the Dutch doll smartly. "You do think yourself a great man, don't you? Ho! And we shall be here far longer than *you* will! Chocolate men only last for a day or two."

The little chocolate man was most astonished.

"What do you mean?" he said, leaning on his chocolate stick and looking hard at the Dutch doll. She laughed, and so did the monkey and the soldier-boy.

"Never you mind!" said the monkey.

"But I do mind!" said the chocolate man. "Tell me what you mean! Of course I shall last longer than a day or two. I shall live for years, like you – till the children are grown up and don't want me any more."

"Well!" said the soldier-boy in surprise. "Do you mean to say that you don't know that chocolate men are meant to be *eaten*?"

There was a long silence. Then the chocolate man cleared this throat and spoke in a trembling voice.

"Eaten! No! I didn't know that – and what's more, I don't believe it!"

"Shh! Here comes Eileen to kiss us goodnight before she goes to bed!" said the Dutch doll. Sure enough the little girl ran across the room and kissed the doll, the soldier-boy and the monkey. She didn't kiss the chocolate man – she suddenly picked him up and bit off half his tall top hat!

"Mummy said I could have a nibble at you tonight, and eat you up tomorrow!"

she said. "Oooh! Your hat does taste nice!" She ran off, and left the toys and the chocolate man alone on the shelf. The chocolate man didn't know whether to be more angry than frightened or more frightened than angry!

"She bit off some of my lovely top hat!" he said. "Oh, the wicked girl! Whatever must I look like?"

"You do look a bit funny," said the monkey sleepily. "But be quiet now and go to sleep."

The chocolate man quickly made up his mind that he wasn't going to stay and be eaten by Eileen. No! He would run away and hide. So, when the three toys on the shelf were fast asleep, he jumped down and ran out of the room.

He came to a passage and looked for somewhere to hide. At the end of it there was a basket with a woolly rug in it. The chocolate man thought he would be nice and comfortable there, so in he hopped, pulled the rug over himself and shut his eyes. Nobody would find him! But the basket belonged to Bobs the dog! And when he came along and curled up there, he sat on the chocolate man and nearly squashed him flat! The poor fellow began to squeak, and Bobs thought it must be a mouse in his basket. Then he smelled a smell of chocolate – and my goodness me, what with thinking of mice and thinking of chocolate too, he went nearly mad with excitement!

He scrabbled round in his basket and snuffled and snorted loudly. The chocolate man was terrified. He leaped out of

the basket and ran down the passage as fast as his chocolate legs would carry him! Bobs went after him – but the chocolate man slipped round a door and hid behind a big basket of eggs. He was in the larder!

Bobs couldn't find him and went back to his basket to sleep. The chocolate man hid by the egg-basket until he thought everything was safe, and then he went exploring in the larder.

He climbed up on to a shelf – and there he met a black-eyed mouse, nibbling at a piece of bacon-rind.

"Hello!" said the mouse, in surprise. "What sort of creature are you?"

"I'm a real slap-up right-to-the-minute chocolate man!" said the chocolate man grandly.

"Then why do you wear only half a hat?" asked the mouse cheekily. The chocolate man was cross at such rudeness and struck the mouse with his chocolate stick. The mouse whipped his tail round and gave the chocolate man such a slash with it that the poor fellow fell headlong into a bowl of milk!

"Ho-ho, ha-ha, he-he!" laughed the mouse, the tears pouring down his cheeks, as he watched the chocolate man floundering about in the milk. The mouse laughed so much that he fell right off the shelf. He fell on to a pile of little cake-tins and they all tumbled down to the floor with a jingling noise!

Almost at once the larder door opened and the cook peered in.

"What's all this noise!" she exclaimed. "It's mice again, I declare! If there isn't one in my bowl of milk."

It wasn't the mouse in the milk, though – it was the poor chocolate man! He just managed to leap out before the cook got hold of him – and he jumped down from the shelf and tore out into the kitchen. The cook raced after him, quite sure he was an extra-big brown mouse.

Round and round the kitchen went the cook and the chocolate man, round and round, round and round. Then, when the little chocolate man was quite puffed out, he spied what looked to him

like a dark cupboard, with the door a
little bit open. In he popped. The cook
didn't see him. She thought he had gone
down a mouse-hole somewhere.

The cupboard was warm, and the little chocolate man felt drowsy after his long scamper. He shut his eyes and went to sleep. The cook went off to bed soon after, and then the house was dark and quiet for the night.

In the morning the chocolate man woke up and stretched himself. He was just going to peep out of his cupboard door when the cook came yawning into the kitchen to light the kitchen fire. She slammed the door round which the chocolate man had been peeping, and then cleared out the fire ready to light it again.

"Oh, well!" thought the little man. "This is a good place here – warm and dark. I shall make it my home! No one will interfere with me here!"

But dear me – he didn't know that it was the oven he had hidden in! Foolish little chocolate man! It grew hot! It grew hotter and hotter . . .

"Very hot today," muttered the chocolate man. "I wish I'd stayed up on that shelf! Very hot – v-v-ery h . . ."

After that he said no more; because he was melting. Soon a dark streak of chocolate ran out of the bottom of the oven door and the cook opened it to see what was the matter.

"Goodness me," she said. "Here's a mess of melted chocolate. Eileen! Did you go and put your chocolate man in the oven? You silly girl – he's all melted now!"

"No, I didn't!" said Eileen. "However could he have got there? He couldn't have got in there by himself, could he?"

Ah, but he could, couldn't he? Well, that was the end of him, poor fellow. It's a warning to all chocolate men not to get into ovens, no doubt about that!

The
Cross Shepherd

Dick wheeled his car out of the shed and got into the driving seat. It was a very nice little car, bright red with silver wheels, and he was very proud of it. It had room for him at the front, and for one more rather small passenger.

The car had a hooter, and two lights in front that you could switch on. Dick worked it with pedals, and could get along very fast indeed. He raced off down the lane at top speed.

"I'm going to see the lambs jumping about in the field!" he called to his mother. "I'll be back in good time for lunch."

He was soon at the big field where the lambs played around the mother sheep. Dick loved to watch them, for they were really very funny. They sometimes jumped on to the top of their mothers – then the big sheep got angry and shook them off.

Dick left his car outside the gate and climbed over into the field. The lambs knew him and came running up. Dick picked one up and cuddled it.

Then a cross voice suddenly came over the field and made Dick jump.

"Put that lamb down! And get out of the field!"

Dick put the lamb down quickly. He looked to see who was shouting, and he saw a bent old shepherd standing at the door of his hut on the other side of the field. The shepherd was waving his stick at Dick as if he meant to hit him with it.

"I wasn't hurting the lamb!" called Dick. "I was only hugging it!"

"You might drop it and break its leg!" shouted back the cross shepherd. "I haven't sat up all night long in the cold winter with my lambs just to let a tiresome boy frighten them and hurt them! You get out of the field – you'll be leaving the gate open next, and letting all the sheep into the road. Be off with you!"

"I couldn't leave the gate open because I always climb over it!" shouted back Dick.

"Now don't you stand there talking to me like that!" said the old shepherd, and he took two or three steps across the field. Dick was really afraid of him, and he ran to the gate, climbed over it, and was soon in his car. He pedalled off down the lane to the hills, thinking that the old shepherd was a very horrid man.

He drove his little car quite a long way, following the paths that ran over the hills. Then he began to feel hungry, so he knew it was time for his lunch.

He pedalled back. It was mostly downhill, so he was soon able to take his feet off the hurrying pedals and put them on the little ledges inside the car, pretending that he really was driving it, just as his father drove the big car.

He came to a little bridge over a stream and stopped for a moment to get out of the car and lean over the side of the bridge to see if there were any fish in the water.

There were no fish – but there was something else! There was a little lamb, struggling to get out of the stream!

"There's a lamb fallen into the water!" said Dick, in surprise. "The banks are so steep just here – it must have been a horrid fall. Poor little thing! Whatever can I do to help it?"

Dick ran down to the side of the
stream. He looked at the water, which
was fairly deep. He could see that the
lamb would soon drown if he did not get
it out. But the banks of the stream were
so steep that it would be very difficult
indeed to reach the lamb.

Dick thought for a moment. No – there
was absolutely nothing else to do but to

jump right into the water, lift up the lamb, and then try to climb out again. He would get very wet but it couldn't be helped.

So into the water he jumped. *Splash!* It was nearly up to his waist! The lamb was caught against an old branch that had fallen into the water and become fixed against the bridge. Dick waded to it.

He lifted the lamb up gently and put it round his neck as he had seen the shepherd do when he wanted to carry a lamb and yet keep his hands free. Then he turned to climb out of the stream. It was very difficult.

He lifted the lamb off his shoulders first and laid it down on the bank. Then he tried to scramble up the steep slope. At last he managed to climb up, and he bent over the lamb.

It could not walk. Dick saw that something had hurt its two front legs. Perhaps they were broken. The lamb lay there looking up at him out of frightened eyes.

"You are begging me for mercy," said Dick, "but you needn't. I only want to help you!"

He put the lamb over his shoulder again, meaning to carry it all the way back to the farm and come back for his car later. But the lamb was well grown and very heavy. Dick knew he couldn't possibly carry it very far. It couldn't walk – so what was he to do?

"I know!" he said suddenly, to the surprised lamb. "You shall be the passenger in my car! I can drive you back easily then."

He put the lamb carefully on the seat next to the wheel. Then he climbed into the driving seat and took hold of the wheel. His wet feet found the pedals and off he went. The lamb lay beside him, feeling more and more surprised, but it trusted this boy with the gentle hands, and was no longer quite so afraid.

People were most astonished to see a lamb as a passenger in Dick's little car! They turned and stared in amazement.

"Did you see that?" they said to one another. "That boy had a lamb in his car!"

"Oh dear!" said Dick to himself, as he pedalled along. "I've got to go and see that cross old shepherd now. I can't just put the lamb into the field and hope he will see it, because he mightn't notice it was hurt, and it does need its legs mended. But surely he would notice by the evening! Shall I just put the lamb through a hole in the hedge and leave it there without saying anything?"

Dick looked at the lamb. It looked back at him. It had a little black nose and wide-staring eyes. Dick liked it very much, and he suddenly knew quite

certainly that he couldn't push the little creature through the hedge and leave it. He must take it to the shepherd, even though he might be shouted at.

He stopped his car outside the gate. He took the lamb in his arms, opened the gate, shut it behind him, and walked over the field towards the shepherd's hut. The sheep set up a great baaing when they saw him, and the old shepherd at once appeared at the door of his hut. When he saw Dick carrying one of the lambs again, he went red with rage.

"Didn't I tell you to leave my lambs alone!" he yelled. "Didn't I tell you to get out of my field! You wait till I catch you, you tiresome boy!"

But Dick didn't run away. He went on towards the shepherd, his heart beating fast. The shepherd raised his stick as if he was going to beat Dick, but the boy called to him.

"Wait! Wait! This lamb of yours is hurt! I found it in the stream, and its legs are hurt. It must have slipped out of the field and run away."

The shepherd at once took the lamb from Dick. He looked at its legs. "They're broken," he said.

"Can you mend them?" asked Dick anxiously.

"They'll mend themselves if I see to them now," said the shepherd. "You can help me if you like."

"Oh, thank you," said Dick. He followed the shepherd into the hut, and

together the two of them gently bound up
the little hurt legs. The shepherd made
clever wooden splints that he bound fast
to each leg. The lamb did not make a
sound, but lay quite still, looking up at
the two who were caring for it.

"You're wet," said the shepherd to
Dick.

"Yes. I had to jump in the stream to get the lamb," said Dick.

"This lamb is heavy," said the shepherd. "Surely you didn't carry it all the way here from the stream?"

"No. I couldn't," said Dick. "I brought it along in my little car. It was my passenger! But I was afraid of bringing the lamb to you because you shouted at me this morning and were very cross."

"Ah! I didn't know then what sort of a boy you were," said the old shepherd. "I get boys in here that break down my hedges and frighten my sheep. So I turn them out of my field. But you can come every day, if you like, and you and I will sit here and watch the lambs playing. I can tell you many a strange tale about lambs and sheep."

"Oh, thank you," said Dick. "Now I must go home to my lunch. I'll come again tomorrow."

"You come and have lunch with me tomorrow," said the old shepherd. "I'll get my wife to make us a picnic lunch, and we'll talk together. I could do with a boy like you for company sometimes!"

Dick went home proudly. The cross shepherd wanted him for a friend! No other boy had ever been able to make friends with the old chap – but Dick could go and have lunch with him the next day.

Now the two are fast friends – and the lamb is quite better. It frisks up to meet Dick when ever it sees the boy coming along in his car – and do you know, it lets him take it for a ride once a week down to the village. It sits beside Dick, just like a proper passenger.

You should see how every one stares!

Little
Mister Sly

Mister Sly lived in a small cottage at the edge of Lilac Village. He kept hens, and sold the eggs, but he never gave any away. He was a mean little fellow, and was only generous when he thought he would get something out of it.

Now one day Sly found six eggs that one of his hens had laid away from the hen-house. He felt sure they had been laid weeks ago, because for at least seven weeks he had shut up his hens carefully, and not let them stray.

"What a pity! They will be bad!" he said to himself. "All wasted!" Then he thought hard. "I could give them away. I'll give them to old Mister Little-Nose. He can't smell anything bad or good since he had the flu last year. Maybe then he will give me some honey from his bees."

So Sly put the eggs into a round basket and took them to Mister Little-Nose.

"Oh, thank you!" said Mister Little-Nose. "That's kind of you, Sly. I will give you some honey in the summertime."

After Sly had gone, Mister Little-Nose heard someone knocking at his door again, and dear me, it was the carrier, bringing twelve eggs for him from his sister.

"Well, well – I've too many eggs now,"

he thought. "I'll send some to the pixie Twinkle."

So he sent his little servant round to Twinkle with the six eggs that Sly had given him. But before Twinkle could use them she had to leave in a hurry to go and see her aunt, who was ill.

"I'll take the eggs to old Dame Groan," she thought. "She's been ill and needs feeding up."

So she took them to Dame Groan's house and left them outside the door, because Dame Groan was asleep. Twinkle could hear her snoring.

Dame Groan grumbled when she saw the eggs. "Twinkle might have known that the doctor has said eggs are the one thing I mustn't eat!" she said. "What a pity! Well, Twinkle is away, so I can't give them back to her. I'll give them to old Miss Scared. She can do with a bit of good luck, she's so poor."

Miss Scared was simply delighted with them. "Oh, thank you, dear Dame Groan," she said. "I do hope you are feeling better now. Thank you very much."

176

But before Miss Scared could eat any of the eggs, there came another knock at her door. She opened it. Outside stood Mister Sly, a horrid, mean look on his face.

"I lent you fifty pence last week," he said. "And you said you would pay me sixty pence back this week. Where is the money?"

"Oh, Mister Sly, I haven't got it. Won't you wait till tomorrow?" said Miss Scared. "Please do."

"Can't wait," said Mister Sly.

Then he caught sight of the six eggs.

"Hello – you've got six eggs! Give me these six eggs, and I'll let you off."

"All right," said poor Miss Scared with a sigh, for she had badly wanted an egg for her tea. "Take them."

Mister Sly went off with the eggs. He didn't know they were the very same old eggs he had taken to Mister Little-Nose that very morning.

"I'll have bacon and eggs for tea," he said, and got out his pan. He put in his bacon and it sizzled well. He put in a few mushrooms – and then he cracked an egg on the side of the pan, and let it run in, among the bacon and mushrooms.

But oh dear, it was bad! Mister Sly managed to scrape it out, and tried another egg. That was bad too. They were all bad! The worst of it was that his bacon tasted of bad egg when he ate it, and the whole kitchen smelled dreadful. Mister Sly felt very sick.

He was very, very angry. "That dreadful Miss Scared!" he said. "How dare she give me bad eggs! This is a matter for the police. I will call Mister

Plod in and tell him all about it. He will give Miss Scared a good talking-to, and that will scare her properly."

So he went to Mister Plod and told him. Then he and Mister Plod went to Miss Scared's cottage and knocked on the door.

"You bad woman! You gave me rotten eggs!" said Sly, angrily. "Where did you get them from?"

"Oh, Dame Groan sent them to me," said Miss Scared, as frightened as could be. "Please, please, don't blame me. I didn't know they were bad. I really didn't."

"Ha – Dame Groan," said Mister Plod, and wrote the name in his notebook. "Come along – we'll go and see her."

So they went to Dame Groan. "Those eggs you gave Miss Scared were bad!" scolded Sly. "How dare you give away rotten eggs?"

"I didn't know they were bad," said Dame Groan, in a rage, "and don't you talk to me like that, Sly. Twinkle sent me those eggs – she said that Mister Little-Nose had given them to her."

"We'll go to Mister Little-Nose then," said Mister Plod. "Ah – there he is, just over there! Hi, Little-Nose, I've got something to ask you."

"What?" said Little-Nose.

"Well, Sly here is trying to trace a batch of bad eggs he had given to him," said Mister Plod. "It seems that Miss Scared gave them to him, and Dame Groan gave them to her, and Twinkle gave them to Dame Groan, and you gave them to Twinkle. Now – did your hens lay them? And what right have you to send out bad eggs?"

"I've got no hens," said Mister Little-Nose, in surprise. "And as for who gave them to me – well, Sly should know, for he sent them round himself!"

"What!" cried Mister Plod, and angrily snapped his notebook shut. "Did you give him six bad eggs, Sly? And you have dared to come and complain to me about them and waste my time, when they were your eggs! You must have known they were bad, too. How dare you, I say?"

Sly hadn't a word to say for himself. Little-Nose looked at him in disgust.

"He always was mean," he said. "He'd never give away anything good. I might have guessed they were bad. Well, I'm glad they came back to you, Sly, very glad. Serves you right!"

And so it did.

Slowcoach
Sammy

Slowcoach Sammy belonged to a family of
brownies, and you can guess why he had
such a funny name. He was such a
slowcoach! He was last in everything, and
his mother, Mrs Trot-About, got quite
cross with him.

"You're always last, Sammy," she said.
"I call the others, and they come running
at once. But you stay behind and make
me feel so cross."

Poor old Slowcoach Sammy! He missed
the bus when he went shopping. He
missed the train when Mrs Trot-About
took the family to see Aunt Twinkle. He
even missed the elephant when he went
to the zoo, so he couldn't have his ride.

One day his mother called to all her
family, "Come with me. I want you to do

183

some gardening. I have lettuce and mustard and cress seeds, and we will plant them all in our garden so that we shall have plenty to eat in the summer."

Tickle came running. Humps rushed up. Jinky came round the corner at top speed. Ricky arrived panting. But Slowcoach Sammy wasn't to be seen, as usual.

"He's watching a spider making its web at the front gate," said Tickle.

"Sammy, Sammy, Sammy! Hurry up or you won't have time to do any gardening!" cried Mrs Trot-About. "I've only twenty minutes to spare to help you all plant your seeds."

But Slowcoach Sammy didn't hurry. He watched the spider till she had finished her web. Then he watched a worm wriggling out of a hole. Then he watched a bird flying right up into the sky. At last he got to his mother and his brothers and sisters.

But they had finished their gardening and were picking up their spades to put them back into the shed.

"What a slowcoach you are, Sammy!" said Mrs Trot-About. "I called you ages ago! Now we have finished, and all the seeds are planted."

"I want to plant some seeds too," said Sammy.

"Well, you can't. The others have planted them all – there they are, neatly labelled in rows," said his mother, waving her spade to the garden beds.

"I do want to plant some seeds!" wept Sammy. "I want some plants of my own too. I do want to plant some seeds!"

"It's no use making that noise," said his mother. "You should have come when you were called. There are no more seeds at all."

Sammy went off to cry in the playroom. He hunted in the cupboard to see if there were any packets of seeds left. And at last he came to a little packet that rattled when he shook it. He opened it. Inside lay a great many tiny coloured round things.

"Seeds!" said Slowcoach Sammy, delighted. "Seeds that everybody else

has forgotten. I'll go and plant them straightaway, and won't the others look blue when they see I have got seeds coming up after all!"

Well, if Sammy had looked closely at that packet, he would have seen that they were tiny beads belonging to his sister Jinky! But he didn't. He just hurried out to plant them.

He made little holes along his garden

bed and shook the beads inside. He covered them up well. He watered them, and patted down the ground nicely. He was very pleased with himself.

"They can call me Slowcoach all they like, but they'll be surprised when they see how much nicer my seeds are than theirs!" said Sammy to himself. "My word, with seeds coloured as brightly as that I ought to have flowers all colours of the rainbow!"

Well, the other seeds began to come up, showing a green mist in the beds – but Slowcoach Sammy's didn't peep through at all! He went out to look

twenty times a day, but it wasn't any use – he didn't see a single green head coming through the soft brown earth.

He was so disappointed. The seeds of the others grew and grew – but Sammy's didn't come up at all. (I'm not really surprised. Are you?)

Mrs Trot-About was sorry to see Sammy so unhappy about his seeds. He had told her that he had found a forgotten packet in the cupboard, and she thought they were mustard and cress or lettuce. She couldn't think why they didn't come up.

"I shall dig them up and see what's the matter with them," said Slowcoach Sammy to the others.

"Maybe they are slowcoaches like you!" said Jinky. They all came with him and watched him dig up his bed. He turned up heaps of the little round coloured things and picked them out of the earth.

"Just look!" he said. "They haven't put out any root or shoot or bud or leaf! What bad seeds they are!"

Then the others began to laugh. How

they laughed! "What's the matter?" asked Sammy, in surprise. "Do you think my seeds are so funny?"

"Yes, we do!" laughed Ricky. "What did you expect to grow from those seeds, Sammy? Necklace flowers and bracelet buds? They are tiny little beads!"

Poor Slowcoach Sammy! He stood and stared at his bead-seeds and tears trickled down his red cheeks. No wonder they wouldn't grow! He had planted beads!

"Never mind, Sammy, you can share my lettuces," said kind Jinky.

"It's not the same to share," said

Sammy. "I want seeds of my own."

"Then you mustn't be such a little slowcoach next time," said his mother. "We'll try and help you not to be."

And what do you think his family say to him when they see Sammy being slow? They say, "Hi, Sammy! Your beads will never grow unless you hurry up!"

Then, my goodness, how he hurries and scurries!